Bethlehem Barn

WRITTEN BY
Debra Westgate-Silva

ILLUSTRATED BY
Marcin Piwowarski

Scripture quotation is from The Authorized Version of the Bible
(The King James' Bible), used by permission of the
Crown's patentee, Cambridge University Press.

Illustrations by Marcin Piwowarski
Book Design by Praise Saflor

Publisher's Cataloging-in-Publication data

Names: Westgate-Silva, Debra, author. | Piwowarski, Marcin, illustrator.
Title: Bethlehem barn / Debra Westgate-Silva; illustrated by Marcin Piwowarski.
Description: Bristol, RI: Luminohr Books, 2023. | Summary: A retelling of the
nativity story from the animals' perspective, inspired by ancient legend that on
Christmas Eve animals are given the gift of speech.

Identifiers: LCCN: 2023936763 | ISBN: 979-8-9881854-0-6 (hardcover) | 979-8-
9881854-1-3 (paperback) | 979-8-9881854-2-0 (ebook)

Subjects: LCSH Christmas—Juvenile fiction. | Domestic animals—Juvenile fiction.
| Animals—Juvenile fiction. | Christmas stories. | BISAC JUVENILE FICTION /
Religious / Christian / Holidays & Celebrations | JUVENILE FICTION / Religious
/ Christian / Animals | JUVENILE FICTION / Holidays & Celebrations / Christmas
& Advent | JUVENILE FICTION / Animals / Farm Animals
Classification: LCC PZ7.1 .W47 Be 2023 | DDC [E]--dc23

For my family,
May the peace, wonder, and true spirit of Christmas
live in your hearts all throughout the year.
—DWS

Ancient legends tell us that for one hour on Christmas Eve, animals are given the gift of speech. If we could have heard the animals on that very first Christmas Eve, what do you think they would have said?

I t was a typical cold winter night as the animals entered the barn.

Cow wanted to eat her hay.

Chicken wanted to check her eggs.

Sheep wished for peace and quiet, but Donkey had just returned from a long journey and wanted to play.

And no one—not a single animal, not even a mouse—noticed Bird up in the rafters puffing her chest preparing to make an announcement.

Everything was as it always was—until Cow reached her food trough.

"What...is...that?"
a wild-eyed Cow bellowed.

"Cow's not speaking Moo!" Donkey exclaimed.

"Donkey, you're not braying," said Chicken.

"Wait. I'm not clucking! Where's my cluck? Where's my cluck?"

"We can talk the way people talk," Donkey shouted. "What fun!"

"All I want is peace and quiet," Sheep grumbled. "Is that too much to ask?"

Cow stomped her foot.

"WHAT'S... THAT... IN... MY... FOOD?"

Up in the rafters, Bird had more important things on her mind. "Excuse me," she called. But no one paid attention.

"Who disturbed Cow's food?" Sheep complained. "You know how she gets when she's hungry."

"Are my eggs in there?" Chicken asked. "Someone keeps moving my eggs."

Donkey scurried closer to Cow. "What is it? What's in there?"

Cow backed away from her trough. "I have no idea."

"Excuse me," Bird repeated. "Excuse me. I have something important—"

"I don't know what THAT is," Donkey interrupted, peering inside. "But I do know it's not your dinner."

Sheep stepped closer. She wanted to know what was happening. Nothing ever kept Cow from her dinner. Nothing ever kept Donkey still.

Soon all the animals crowded around the trough.

Up in the rafters, Bird took a deep, calming breath. "That's what I've been trying to tell you," she said slowly. "There's a baby in—"

"Baby?" Cow backed away. "Not my baby! Calves don't look like that."

"That never happened to my eggs before," said Chicken.

"A baby!" Donkey clicked his heels together in the air and shouted, "Can we keep him?"

"It's a human baby," Bird said.

"A human baby!" Cow repeated. "How did he get here?"

Sheep looked around. "Where there's a human baby, there's usually a human grown-up nearby."

"The grown-up is right here." Bird flew from the rafters and hovered above a nearby mound of hay. Barely visible, a woman slept, hidden in the hay for warmth. "The man has gone for provisions. Now, what I've been trying to tell you—"

"Why is her baby in my food?"
Cow demanded.

"WOULD YOU PLEASE LISTEN!"

Bird hollered.

All the animals froze,
for Bird never spoke
above a chirp.

"The baby," Bird continued with a deep breath, "is the one the holy men talk about, the one the people sing about when I go to temple."

A stunned silence filled the barn.

"This?" Chicken asked. "This is The One?"

"Such a great one would not be in our simple barn," Cow said.

"The prophets said He would be wrapped in swaddling clothes," Bird reminded them. "They said He would be lying in a manger."

The animals studied the sleeping infant.

"He's wrapped in swaddling clothes," Chicken finally said. "He's lying in a manger."

"A star," Sheep said. "You told us they spoke of a star."

Bird nodded knowingly and gestured to the door.

Cow, Chicken, and Sheep bolted to the door and thrust their heads out, and there, filling the night sky with its brilliance, shone a star brighter than all the others.

"Truly?" Cow asked. "This little one is the one whose coming has been foretold throughout the ages?"

Bird bowed her head. "The prophets told us what we'd see. This is it. This is the people's savior."

"The King of Kings?" Cow asked.

"The Prince of Peace," Chicken said.

"The Lamb of God," Sheep whispered.

Only Donkey had remained silent throughout this, lost in his own thoughts.

"What is it, Donkey?" Chicken asked.

"I carried them," he said slowly, "from Nazareth to Bethlehem. I didn't mind their talk then, but I understand now. They spoke of an angel."

"An angel?" the animals repeated.

"Yes," Donkey nodded excitedly. "The man said an angel came to him and told him that the child will be a boy and to name him Jesus. He will save the people from their sins."

"I carried them," Donkey repeated, straightening.

"I walked
    steady and tall,
over hills and
    across desert,
never playing
    at all. I carried
    the baby
Jesus!"

Donkey seemed to grow in importance right before their eyes.

Cow, Chicken, and Sheep looked from the baby to Donkey and back again.

Suddenly, the barn burst into frenzied activity.

Cow grabbed all the hay she could carry from the fresh bales. Chicken ran to and fro waving her wings wildly. Sheep scratched furiously against a wooden post.

A whirlwind of hay, feathers,

and
wool
swirled
through
the
air.

When the dust and hay and feathers and wool settled, the manger was fluffed with Cow's freshest hay. A pillow of Chicken's softest feathers now cushioned the infant's head, and blankets fashioned from tufts of Sheep's wool warmed mother and child.

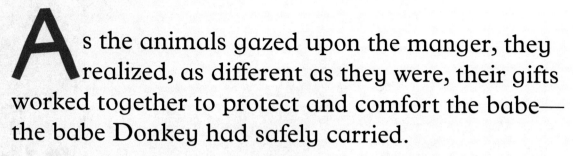

As the animals gazed upon the manger, they realized, as different as they were, their gifts worked together to protect and comfort the babe— the babe Donkey had safely carried.

Donkey brayed softly.

Sheep bleated in return.

Chicken gave a contented cluck.

Cow let out a satisfied moo, and Bird burst into a song of praise.

Together, they knelt to honor baby Jesus and to guard and warm Him through the cold winter night.

It was a glorious night in the barn, as peace and great joy descended upon them all.

"Glory to God in the highest, and on earth peace, good will toward men."

Luke 2:14 KJV

Discussion Questions:

- Which animal was your favorite? Why?
- How many times did you spot the little mouse in the illustrations?
- How did the animals know who Jesus was?
- Jesus is known by many different names in the Bible. Which names were used in the story? What are some others?
- What did each animal do or give to keep baby Jesus warm and safe?
- Just like each animal helped baby Jesus, we can all show kindness and bring comfort to others. What can you do to make your community a better place?
- Why do you think a cat and a mouse are sleeping near each other in the last picture?
- Many people believe animals were witness to Jesus' birth. What can you do to celebrate the animals this Christmas?
- How can you share the good news about Jesus and Christmas?

For activities and ideas
—and to see what other young people are doing—
visit my website at
www.debrawestgatesilva.com
or scan the QR code below.

About the Author

Debra Westgate-Silva has worked in public education for many years and in child advocacy and welfare. Her work has been published in *Highlights* children's magazine, *Teaching Tolerance,* and *Intrepid Times.* She loves reading, writing, cooking (and eating!), traveling and, above all else, spending time with her family. Her favorite holiday is Christmas, and one of her most treasured traditions is baking a birthday cake each year for baby Jesus. She lives in Bristol, Rhode Island, with her husband and two sons. Please visit her website at www.debrawestgatesilva.com to send her a message. She also loves to hear from her readers!

About the Illustrator

Marcin Piwowarski is a self-taught artist in traditional and digital illustration. He has pursued both an international and domestic career in painting and children's book illustration and has illustrated hundreds of books during his artistic journey. His artwork is inspired by nature, daily life, and music, mixing the magical and mysterious with down-to-earth elements of everyday reality. Marcin lives in Poland with his three children. Check out his Instagram and Facebook to see more of his work.

Made in the USA
Las Vegas, NV
11 November 2023

80617706R00019